To Henry

From...Gigi........Papa

♡

It was Christmas Eve and Henry
was snug and warm in his cozy bed.
He was trying so hard to go to sleep.
But he could hear strange noises.

It wasn't the sound of sleigh bells.
It wasn't the sound of reindeer hoofs on the roof.
It wasn't even the sound of Santa unpacking his sack.

It was more of a

HARUMPH!

and an

OOF!

It was no use.

There'd be no sleep for Henry
until he'd found out what
was making that noise.

Henry crept down the stairs
and peered into the living room.
There were three stockings
hanging from the fireplace.

One of them belonged to
Henry. But where had the
other two come from?
Suddenly, a muffled voice
came from the chimney.

"Oh, dear.
I'm even
more
stuck now!"

There was a scuffling sound from behind the Christmas tree, and Henry jumped as a small elf appeared.

"Uh, hello," said the elf. "I guess you've caught us!"

Henry listened as the elf explained
that Santa was stuck in the chimney.
The elf had tried to pull him out. But the
only things that had come down so far
were Santa's boots and pants!

"I can help you," suggested Henry. "I'll hold Santa's feet and we can both pull."
The elf agreed. "Between us, we might be able to get him unstuck."

Henry grasped both of Santa's feet firmly.
But, just at that moment, a light went on upstairs.
"Henry, is that you?" called his mom. "Back to
bed now, please, or Santa won't come!"

At that exact moment,
Santa shot back up
the chimney... with
Henry still hanging
onto his feet.

The poor elf could not believe his eyes.
But there was no time to think...
Henry's mom was coming
out of her bedroom.

"I'm coming!" squeaked the elf. He hurried
up the stairs and jumped into Henry's
bed, pulling the covers up over his head.
"Night-night, sweetie!" said Henry's
mom through the doorway.

Meanwhile, up on the roof, Santa and Henry had landed in a heap. The clever reindeer had hooked their reins under Santa's arms and pulled as hard as they could.

"Good job!" said Santa, brushing himself down. "No more cookies for me tonight!"

Henry scrambled to his feet. But Santa was so busy, he didn't notice that Henry and the elf had traded places!

"I think we'd better deliver the rest of the presents first," said Santa, "and leave this house for last."

Santa wasn't really listening.
He was talking to the reindeer.
"Up, up, and away!" Santa called,
and the reindeer took off before
Henry had time to explain.

Henry held on tight as the
sleigh climbed high into the
night sky, above the rooftops.

Surrounded by sacks, Henry was so busy figuring out which presents were which, there was no time to let Santa know that there'd been a mistake.

There were **big** presents for the cities,

and **SHINY** presents for the towns.

There were **ODD**-shaped presents for the villages,

and **mystery** presents for the farms.

To Henry

As they landed at their next stop, Santa decided that he couldn't risk getting stuck in a chimney again.

"Elf, I think you'd better make the deliveries from now on," decided Santa, "while I sort the presents."

Henry *shimmied* down chimneys.

He **squeezed** through cat flaps.

And, if all else failed, he used Santa's *magic* key to let himself in.

In each house, Henry picked up the cookies to take home to Mrs. Claus, and carrots for the reindeer.

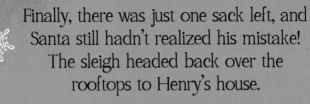

Finally, there was just one sack left, and
Santa still hadn't realized his mistake!
The sleigh headed back over the
rooftops to Henry's house.

Henry had never had so much fun as when he slid down his own chimney with a sack of his own presents.

He put his presents under the Christmas tree, then picked up Santa's pants and boots and put them in the sack.

"Psst! Elf, where are you?" whispered Henry.

A very happy Elf appeared, rubbing his eyes. "I've had such a lovely nap," he said. Henry handed over the sack and waved as Elf disappeared up the chimney.

Back in his cozy bed, Henry listened to the sounds of reindeer hoofs on the roof, sleigh bells, and, very faintly,

"Ho ho ho!
Merry Christmas!"

Or was that,

"Ho ho ho!

yummy cookies!"?

Write your name on the gift tags.

Draw yourself as an elf.

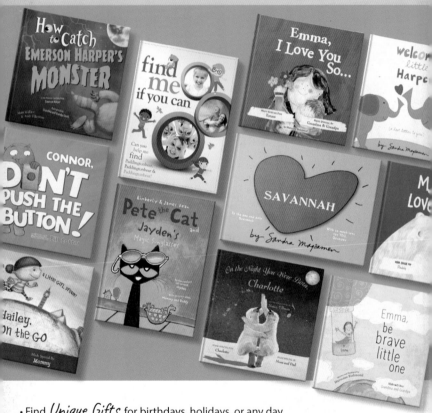